ELEPHANT AT THE DOOR

DON CONROY

POOLBEG

FOR CHILDREN

Published 1997
by Poolbeg Press Ltd
123 Baldoyle Industrial Estate
Dublin 13, Ireland

Reprinted November 1997
Reprinted December 1998
Reprinted November 2000

© Don Conroy 1997

The moral right of the author has been asserted.

A catalogue record for this book is available from the British Library.

ISBN 1 85371 881 5

Illustrations by Don Conroy
Cover design by Poolbeg Group Services Ltd
Set by Poolbeg Group Services Ltd in Times 16/24
Printed by The Guernsey Press Ltd,
Vale, Guernsey, Channel Islands.

For Sophie

About the Author

Don Conroy is a well-known writer of children's fiction, television personality and an enthusiastic observer of wildlife. He sketches animals and birds native to Ireland and is one of Ireland's best-loved writers and illustrators for children. *The Anaconda from Drumcondra* is also available in this series.

D id you ever make a wish? One that came true?

Well, I did. Really! I'm not kidding!

Now, I know there are special times for making a wish. If you see a shooting star is one, throwing a coin into a fountain is another, and so is finding a four-leafed clover. If a leaf falls on your head, or a black cat crosses your path . . . some people consider these things unlucky, especially if you're American, but I'm not.

1

Of course, when it's your birthday you make a wish while blowing out the candles; this is always a good one. Mmm . . . I'm trying to remember some more. Yes, you can make a wish when you throw a coin into a fountain or a wishing-well.

Well, mine was very simple, an occasion that you might come across most Sundays at mealtime. Have you guessed yet? Right first time. A wishbone from a chicken.

Oops, silly of me, I never introduced myself. My name is Sophie Richardson. Well, I was telling you about my wish coming true . . .

It all happened when the family went to visit Gran on her birthday. That's Dad's mum. She was celebrating her eightieth birthday. Dad wanted to take her out to lunch but Gran preferred to stay at home and have the family visit her. Mum agreed. She thought it was a better idea than going out to a restaurant. Gran always says they give her far too much food. She hates waste and she always gets indigestion if she eats all that's on her plate.

Hee! Hee! Ha! Ha! Ho! Ho! . . . the last time we were all in a restaurant together . . . Hee! Hee! Hee! . . .

Gran complained that there was enough food on her plate to feed her and four of her bridge friends . . . Dad suggested getting a doggy-bag after the meal.

"You know I don't have a dog," she retorted.

3

Everyone broke into laughter when she said this. Mum then explained the reason for the doggy-bag.

Then Gran broke into hoots of laughter. "Oh, I am very silly!" she giggled.

Soon she had nearly everyone in the restaurant laughing with her. I didn't know about doggy-bags either until Robert told me. More about him later.

For Gran's birthday I bought her a book, a detective story. Well, it was three books in one actually, and it had large type to help her read more easily. Robert bought lavender perfume for her – Mum said it was her favourite.

By the way, Mum's name is Lucy and Dad's is Edward, but everyone calls him Teddy. Mum and Dad bought her a new toaster. She loves toast and marmalade in the morning with a nice pot of tea. She has a lovely tea cosy for her teapot that she knitted herself, before I was even born.

I am eight and a half years old, if you are wondering.

My brother Robert, who is a bit of a pain most of the time, is eleven. He loves anything to do with sport but that's not what makes him a pain. 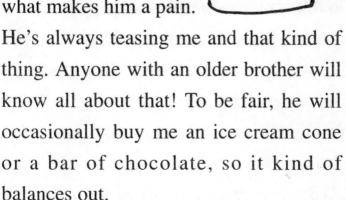 He's always teasing me and that kind of thing. Anyone with an older brother will know all about that! To be fair, he will occasionally buy me an ice cream cone or a bar of chocolate, so it kind of balances out.

My mum is one of those busy people always doing things – she just cannot relax, except when she's reading a book or doing a crossword. My dad would play and talk golf all day if he got the chance. He even says to Mum "It's business!" as he hurries to a golf course, whatever "It's business!" means.

Is there anything else you should know before you hear this amazing story? Oh yes, just a few other things so you get the picture. We, the Richardsons, live in a nice semi-detached house about a mile from the sea. We have a canary called Bird, a cat called Kitty, Kitty – which can be very confusing to other cats when we call her name – and a dog called Ezra Hound.

As you can guess, I didn't think up

any of those names. Dad is to blame for all of them. When we have a visitor coming for the first time, Dad can't wait to introduce the animals. The dog's name always gets a laugh. Hopefully, the poor dog won't develop a complex, since people laugh at it all the time. Mum explained it once . . . something to do with poetry, or a poet. That's another thing Dad likes – poetry! How very odd, don't you agree?

There's one thing that must be mentioned that's very important to the story. I'm a collector. Some people collect stamps, toy cars, badges, soft toys . . . one of my friends collects anything to do with owls and pigs. Another friend collects dolphins; not real ones, of course! I, on the other hand, collect everything to do with elephants. I just love elephants. Yes, it's a bit unusual, I know. Most people collect dolls or teddies, but they never really interested me. It had to be elephants.

I have often tried to figure out when my interest in pachyderms began. *Pachyderm* is a fancy name for elephants, hippos and rhinos. Mum told me that one – she probably got it from one of the general knowledge crosswords that she and Gran love to do. Anyway, it was around the time I went to the circus and was allowed to sit on an elephant's back and had my photograph taken on it. Which I still have in a frame on my dressing-table. I was only four at the time, but I'll never forget the excitement of it.

I have posters on my bedroom walls of African elephants, Asian ones, even woolly mammoths that roamed the world ages ago. I have a gold charm bracelet with tiny elephants and I also have soft toys, badges, T-shirts, playing cards, books, stickers – even a purple elephant-shaped soap.

I find elephants so fascinating! They are the biggest creatures in the world. Well, on the land, I mean. And do you know something that they cannot do? Now, not like make a telephone call or drive a car, or that sort of thing. Something that is natural to most other animals? Give up?

Jump! Believe it or not, elephants can't jump. Oh, that's another thing . . . I record any wildlife film shown on television with elephants. You might think I'm a bit spoiled but I'm not really.

Now, back to elephants. Can you imagine the alphabet without E for Elephant? You see how important they are.

Well, there we all were, sitting around the table on the Sunday of Gran's birthday. Dad carved the free-range chicken and, when Gran got the wishbone, she insisted that I pull it with her.

"Pull hard, Sophie, darling," said Gran, as she curled her little finger around one side of the V-shaped bone. I grabbed the other side. I wanted Gran to win because it was her birthday. Gran quickly sensed what I was up to. "Come on, Sophie, you can do better than that," she coaxed. I pulled harder this time and got the bigger part of the bone which, as you know, meant I had to make the wish. Gran clapped her hands. "Well done! Well done!"

I begged Gran to make the wish since she was the birthday person. Robert pulled a face and glared upwards, then mimicked me saying: *I want you to have my wish 'cos it's your birthday.* Dad laughed at his excellent impersonation.

"Make your wish," said Gran, "but don't tell anyone."

Well, I made my wish in secret and, of course, you can guess what I wished for.

"Well, what did you

wish for?" asked Robert. I wasn't going to tell him.

"I suppose you wished for a big elephant so you can bring it home and cuddle it. and show all your little friends, saying 'Look what I got making a wish!'" he sniggered.

"That's enough teasing," said Mum, jumping to my defence.

I pulled an ugly face at him and stuck out my tongue as far as it could go, making sure only Robert saw me.

"Time for the birthday cake," said Mum.

"We won't put on all the candles," said Dad. "We don't want the heat to keep us away."

Gran laughed and gave him a friendly push that nearly knocked him off his chair.

"Happy Birthday To You, Happy Birthday To You . . ." Mum sang as she walked in from the kitchen with the lovely cake. "Sophie, go quickly and bring in the small plates for the cake."

As I went to get the plates I heard the letterbox flip up. It must be some more birthday cards for Gran, I thought. Then I remembered it was Sunday and the postman doesn't deliver on Sundays. I peered around the door of the kitchen and you will never believe what I saw coming through the letterbox.

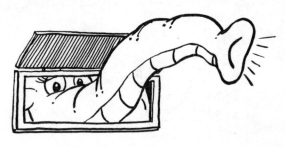

It was an elephant trunk! Well, I can tell you, I got such a shock I nearly dropped the plates. It began to swing from side to side like some demented snake. Then it quickly shot back through the letterbox.

I shook my head, thinking I must be dreaming, then hurried back in with the plates.

"Oh what lovely cake!" said Gran. "You will all have to help me blow these candles out."

"Go on, Gran," said Robert. "You can do it."

"I'll give it a go," she smiled, patting her chest.

We watched Gran drawing in a big lungful

of air like she meant to blow the whole house down. My eyes nearly popped out for I could see the elephant's trunk again at the half-open window, just beside where Gran was sitting.

Suddenly, there was a big gust of wind that not only blew out the candles but sent several strawberries and dollops of cream over Dad.

"Wow!" said Robert. "What powerful lungs you have, Gran."

Mum was pointing at Dad, laughing hysterically as he wiped the

15

cream that covered his face and hair.

"Oops, I'm dreadfully sorry, darling," said Gran to Dad, chuckling. "I don't know my own power."

Dad didn't look too pleased as most of the cream was on his favourite golf shirt. But he laughed it off, saying he wasn't expecting the first piece of the cake. I looked at the half-open window and saw the elephant's face quite clearly. It was smiling back at me, then it gave me the biggest wink I had ever seen and disappeared. I reached up my hand to point towards the window.

"Don't be greedy!" said Robert, thinking I was reaching for the cake. "Gran should get the first slice."

"There you are, Gran," said Mum,

passing over the slice of cake and giving me a disapproving glance.

"Would you look out the window, Dad? I thought I saw something unusual outside the window."

Dad looked puzzled, but craned his head over to investigate. "Oh my goodness," he gasped recoiling as if he'd seen a monster. "Yes, there is something very strange indeed. It's trying to fly. Aah!"

"What is it?" I asked, becoming alarmed. "Is it an elephant?"

"It's a jumbo sized pair of bloomers blowing on the line," he exclaimed.

"Ted," said Mum. "You're terrible." She gave an embarrassed laugh.

"He's such a joker, that son of mine," said Gran. "Just like his dear father."

"No elephants?" said Robert, sniggering at me.

"Time to open your presents," said Mum.

"Oh, goody," said Gran. "I simply love presents." She opened the present from Robert. "Oh lovely, lavender cologne, my favourite. I shall smell wonderful all year. Thank you, honey. Give your old granny a hug." Robert hugged her awkwardly.

"You spoil me," she giggled as she unwrapped another present. "Ah, Agatha Christie's thrillers. Wonderful.

I'll know how to commit the perfect crime after this," she whispered in mock-sinister tones.

Gran reached over and hugged me warmly. "You clever girl, to pick the right book for me."

"Well, Mum helped me choose it," I admitted.

Then the biggest present was handed to her. "Here Gran. Close your eyes."

"Oh, I feel like a child again," she giggled and unwrapped the paper to reveal a rectangular cardboard box. Still with her eyes closed she felt the box, picked it up and shook it, saying, "The suspense is killing me." Opening her eyes, she could see it was a toaster. "Oh, Lucy, Ted, it's just what I need. That old toaster of mine is only fit for the rubbish tip. No more trying to make toast under the grill."

"It's got a space for four slices," said Dad proudly as he took it out of the box. "You can invite all your bridge friends over for breakfast."

"Well, I'm so pleased with all the wonderful gifts, and now I'll put the kettle on for a nice cup of tea."

"No," said Mum. "It's your day off, Gran."

"Can I make it?" I offered. "I know to heat the teapot and use tea leaves 'cos Gran prefers them."

"You *are* a clever girl," said Gran.

I hurried out to the kitchen, filled the kettle, then plugged it in. While I was waiting for it to boil, I quickly opened the kitchen door to the garden to check whether I had really seen an elephant or if it was just my vivid imagination.

I could see nothing unusual in the garden, only a blackbird having a bath in the small fish-pond. I checked around by the shed. Nothing there. I began to think I'd been seeing things, so back I went into the kitchen. I made the tea, put cups, milk, sugar, biscuits and the teapot on a tray and was about to carry them into the dining-room when a head popped out from the broom cupboard.

"Hi, Sophie. Any chance of getting me a slice of that delicious cake?"

I got such a shock I nearly let the tray drop. The elephant quickly caught it with his trunk. "Some people call me the fastest trunk in town. Hee! Hee! Just kidding," the elephant smiled warmly.

"Who are you?" I asked.

"My name is Archie. I live in wishland. Some people call it dreamland or wonderland. It has lots of cute names." He started to sing. "Somewhere over the rainbow . . ."

"Shush, they'll hear you." I cautioned. "But how did you get here?"

"Don't you remember you wished for me?" Archie said anxiously. "As you know, elephants never forget," he said, putting his trunk around my waist. "That's what's called an elephant hug." The front of the trunk ran up Sophie's spine in a ticklish fashion. "Have an itch you need to scratch?" he chuckled.

"No." I couldn't help laughing. "Listen, I'd better bring this tea to Gran."

"Good thinking," said the elephant. "Don't forget the cake!"

"I won't," I promised.

"Who were you talking to?" asked Robert.

"An elephant, of course, who else?" I retorted. "May I have another slice of that delicious cake, Gran?"

"Of course, my dear."

This time Gran cut off a really big slice for me and offered some more to the others. I made to leave the room.

"Where are you going?" asked my brother.

"I'm just checking that I didn't leave the tap running."

I quickly headed back into the kitchen and opened the broom cupboard. No sign of the elephant. I looked out the window into the garden: he was not there either. Then the fridge door opened.

"Boo!" said the elephant. "I was just cooling off." He pushed me gently. I went crashing into the door. "Oops, sorry about that. I don't know my own strength sometimes."

"I'm all right," I said. "My brother is much rougher than that."

"Would that delicious-looking slice of cake with the strawberries on top belong to a certain talented pink elephant?"

"It would," I laughed.

"Thanks!" The elephant snatched the cake and quickly polished it off. Then he began to lick the tip of his trunk like you'd lick your fingers.

"Delicious!" he remarked. Putting his trunk around me again, he said, "How do you know there's been an elephant in the fridge? Footprints in the jelly!" Archie started bellowing with laughter.

"Quiet, they'll hear."

"You're right. You and I are the only ones who know about me, right?"

"Right. Let's keep it that way for the present until I can find some way of explaining you. I'd better go back inside."

"Sure thing, mum's the word," said the elephant. "Or, in this house, should I say 'Gran's the word'? I just *kill* me." He chuckled again.

I pressed his trunk across his mouth. "Quiet! Please!"

"Oh yes, quiet. Oh, by the way . . ." said the elephant, looking very guilty. "There was jelly in the fridge. Raspberry. It was scrumptious. Slipped down a treat. And the ice cream . . . I hope Gran doesn't mind."

I thought I'd slip out later and buy more ice cream and jelly with my pocket money to replace it.

"Would you like some jelly?" asked Gran as I returned.

I could feel myself blushing. "You

have a very guilty look on your face," said Mum. "What is it?"

"Well, Gran, I helped myself to the jelly and ice cream already."

"You're supposed to ask when you're in other people's houses," snapped Robert.

"Sure, she's in her granny's," laughed Gran. "No one has to ask around here."

"I'll do the washing-up," I offered.

"Feeling guilty, are we?" said my brother slyly.

"Yes, that's a good idea," said Mum. "And you can help, Robert."

"Why should I? I didn't steal things from the fridge."

"I'd prefer to do it on my own," I snapped.

"Let's sit down in the sitting-room," suggested Gran. "I've a lovely box of chocolates that my bridge friends gave me."

"Gran, I'm stuffed to the gills," said Dad. "But I wouldn't mind watching the match; it's the semifinal of the World Cup."

"Football," sighed Mum. "I can't understand what all the fuss is about. It's only men kicking a ball of air about a pitch."

They all moved in to the sitting-room.

I looked at all the washing-up, piled high. I hadn't realised there was so much. "If only Gran had a dishwasher," I sighed.

"Hello again," said the elephant. "I see

you're on the washing-up . . . never mind, I'll help." He quickly picked the basin from the drainer and filled it, first with hot, then cold water. "Too hot!" he yelled, as he dipped his trunk into the water. He turned on the cold tap and tested the temperature again. "Ah, that's better." Then, squeezing the washing-up liquid into the water he swirled it about until it bubbled up. "Bubbles," he smiled. "I simply love bubbles. Do you want to see me blow the biggest bubble ever?"

"We're supposed to be doing the washing-up."

"Just one, OK?" He tickled me under the chin with his trunk.

"Well, OK," I said. I really wanted to see could he blow a giant bubble.

The elephant stuck his trunk into the washing-up water and siphoned up all the water, then began to burp and hiccough. "Oops, pardon! Hic . . ."

Bubbles started popping out everywhere from the elephant's trunk and mouth. Tiny ones, large round ones, long narrow ones. "Hic! Hic!" The kitchen was filling with bubbles. As soon as one would pop, another would appear.

I just couldn't help laughing as I watched the elephant holding his breath in an attempt to stop burping and hiccoughing. The minute he'd let out his breath again, hundreds of bubbles would escape from his trunk. "Try making the one big one that you said you'd make," I suggested.

"That's a very good idea. Hic . . ." The elephant held his breath again then slowly released it. The biggest bubbles I have ever seen began to come out of the elephant's trunk. Then they joined together, making a bubble that began to fill the entire kitchen. It was pouring into every nook and cranny of the room, pressing me against the wall, and still it seemed to be getting bigger and bigger like a hot-air balloon. Soon it would pour out into the other rooms. I couldn't let that happen, so I picked up the kitchen scissors and burst it. There was a very loud "pop" and it was gone.

"I think that's enough bubbles for one day," said Archie sheepishly.

"Definitely," I said.

"Hic . . . hic . . ."

"Oh, no," I said, as more bubbles began to pour out from his mouth and trunk.

"Sorry, Sophie, I can't stop them."

"How do you stop the hiccoughs?" I wondered out loud, thinking fast. The elephant was trying to hold his breath to stop the hiccoughs, but it wasn't working. Then I remembered that frightening someone could stop them.

"Aahh!" I screamed loudly. "A mouse!" pointing to the elephant's feet.

Archie let out a loud trumpeting noise and jumped up on the table. "Where? Where is it?" He stood there trembling.

"I was just joking," I said. Archie looked puzzled. "If you frighten someone, it helps to cure their hiccoughs."

"No need to scare me half to death,"

he complained. "Wait a minute . . . it worked! My hiccoughs are gone. Thank you, Sophie. That was clever! You have permission to frighten the wits out of me anytime I have hiccoughs."

"I thought elephants couldn't jump," I retorted.

"Well, I'm not your average elephant-type. I can jump, dance, fly, sing . . ."

He was just about to sing "Nellie the Elephant" when Dad hurried to the kitchen. "What's going on in here? The washing-up hasn't even been started . . . and what is that elephant doing on the table?" He looked again. "An elephant!!!" He fainted with shock.

"Oh dear, now look what you've done!" I sighed.

"Never fear," said the elephant. Turning on the cold tap, he took a big drink of water. He pointed his trunk at Dad, who was lying on his back on the floor. "Ready, aim, fire!"

The water shot out from his trunk like water from a hose and drenched Dad. He began to come round but, when he saw the elephant, he fainted again.

"Your dad is easily shocked," said Archie. "I mean, it's not as if I were a cobra." His trunk began to move about like a snake. "Or a grizzly bear." With that, he pulled himself up on his hind legs and began to growl.

"I think I'd better call Mum," I said.

"Good idea," said the elephant.

Dad was gently revived by Mum tapping him lightly on the face. "Where am I?" he wondered.

"You just fainted, dear," she said.

"I thought I saw an elephant in the kitchen," he laughed, hysterically. "Isn't that silly?"

"You did, darling," she said calmly.

"I did?" He fainted again.

"Oh dear, that's the third time he's done that," I sighed.

It was six o'clock before Dad came round.

"Feeling better, dear?" asked Gran.

"I recorded the match for you," said Robert.

Gran put down her knitting and said brightly, "It's time for tea. I'll make toast with my lovely new present." She smiled broadly.

"But . . . but . . . " stuttered Dad. "There's an elephant on the sofa watching TV."

"That's right, dear," said Gran. "And it helped Sophie do all the washing-up after lunch."

"But can you see it?" he asked Mum in disbelief.

"Yes, dear. Archie really enjoyed watching the match."

"Archie? Is everybody gone nuts around here? There's an elephant in the room and you're all so calm about it!"

"Surely you must have wished for something special when you were a boy?" said Mum. "I know I did. I remember wishing for a rag-doll with a long dress. Next morning, there it was on my bed. I was *so* happy."

Gran added, "Yes, I remember you wished for a leather football and you got it."

"Listen," said Dad. "We're not talking dolls or footballs, but an elephant!"

"Surely she can wish for anything she wants," said Mum. "You know how much Sophie likes them."

"Hi," said Archie, waving his trunk in a friendly gesture.

"It can talk!" said Dad, even more alarmed.

"Well, he's not exactly your average,

normal type of elephant," said Robert. "More of a figment of someone's imagination." He pointed at me.

"Exactly!" nodded the elephant. "I'm what you call a bit of a figment. A big one, of course," he chuckled.

"Well, this figment of my daughter's imagination is sitting on that sofa!"

"It's exciting, isn't it?" I said.

"I can't believe how you're all taking it so lightly."

"It's very light indeed," said Gran. "It can make itself as light as a feather . . . show him, like a good elephant."

Archie began to float upwards towards the ceiling then, flapping his ears, he began to fly around the room. "Look everybody, I'm Dumbo," said the elephant. "And I'll work for peanuts. Hee! Hee!"

"He can also make himself very heavy," said Robert.

"No, I don't want to see that," said Dad. "I don't want a hole in the floor.

Now, would you ask him to please come down again, gently?"

The elephant glided down and landed lightly on the sofa. "Perfect landing, don't you agree?" he smiled.

"He's very good at general knowledge," said Gran. "He was a great help with my Sunday crossword."

"I've never heard anything so ridiculous in all my life," snapped Dad.

"Well, if you're so clever," said Mum, "tell Gran what Carthaginian general crossed the Alps in 218 B.C."

Dad looked blank.

"You'd know it if it was a question about golf," Robert teased.

"Well, let's hear elephant Einstein answer that one," Dad grumbled.

"Easy-peasy," said the elephant. "Hannibal, and he crossed the Alps with fifty-seven African elephants."

"Hannibal fits," said Gran. "That's the first time in a month I've completed the crossword." She got up and gave the elephant a big hug then headed for the kitchen.

"Ah, gee, it was nothing," beamed Archie.

"I still can't get over someone wishing up an elephant," said Dad.

"It could be worse," Mum laughed. "She might have wished for a dinosaur."

"Yes," said Robert. "That would have been deadly, a *Tyrannosaurus Rex,* for instance."

"No thanks, I'm happy with my elephant," I said, cuddling the big soft creature.

"I remember one little boy wishing for a dragon," said the elephant. "Luckily his dad worked in the fire brigade. Still, it was handy for lighting fires in wintertime – they never had to buy matches."

"Tea's ready!" said Gran.

We all sat around having toast and raspberry jam and fruitcake. Poor Dad still found it difficult to accept the fact that an elephant was sitting at the table with the family and pouring out tea for everyone.

Later that evening, when we arrived home, Dad stopped at the front door. "Now, let's get one thing straight, young lady. That thing  there," he pointed to Archie as I helped him out of the boot of the car, "is not coming into the house. Understood?"

"But, Dad . . ." I pleaded. "We can't leave him outside. He has no place to sleep."

"He's an elephant," said Dad. "Let him act like one and sleep outdoors. And that's final."

"I'm sorry, I can't bring you inside," I tried to console Archie.

"Oh, I'll be fine, sleeping

out under the stars, feeling the fresh air."
He took a big gulp of air and shivered. "Of
course, it's a bit cloudy," he said, looking
up at the sky. "And there's a slight nip in
the air. It might rain or snow or worse,
but don't worry about me, I'll be fine."

I gave him a big hug and went inside.
Dad sat down on the sofa, not looking
too pleased. Mum sat beside him,
reading a book, smiling to herself. I
watched television for a short time then
went up to my room.

Soon there was a tap, tap, tap on the

glass of my bedroom window. I could

see the elephant's trunk. Archie had floated up to the window. I opened it. "Are you all right?" I asked.

"Well, I wouldn't mind watching some tv. It's a bit boring sitting out on the grass. The dog won't play with me, he's too frightened. I suppose I'm to blame, really. When he returned from his walk in the park with Robert, he found me in his kennel. Even the cat is in a sulk with me. When I was trying to sleep, she pounced on me. Thinking she wanted to play, I lifted her up with my trunk and swung her about several times by the tail. She got most offended; just padded off, hissing and snarling. Still, I had some fun with the canary: it has a lovely song you know. But your dad saw this, and put a cover over the cage and closed the window."

"Don't blame Dad too much. It takes some getting used to, having an elephant around the place."

"Yes, I suppose you're right," remarked Archie. "Well, I can tell you something, Sophie. I don't think I'll ever get used to people. They're so different to elephants."

"Would you like to watch some wildlife videos?" I asked.

"Splendid idea."

"We'll go to my brother's room. He has a video and TV there. I'm sure he won't mind if it's for you."

Robert agreed. He sneaked downstairs, put on a pizza and later the three of us

sat on the bed, eating pizza and watching wildlife programmes. Archie reduced himself in size (another of his tricks!) so the three of us could sit comfortably on the bed. We sat there for hours until we all felt very tired.

"You can stay in my room," I said to Archie, "but you must be very quiet."

We tiptoed out of one bedroom into the other. I got into my nightie then went into the bathroom to brush my teeth. Archie followed me, but forgot he'd made himself bigger again and got stuck in the door.

"Ouch!" he said, as he tried to squeeze himself into the bathroom.

"What's the matter?" I asked, with a mouthful of toothpaste.

"I'm stuck!"

"Well, make yourself thinner or smaller," I said.

"Oh yes, I forgot," said Archie. Then he whispered to me, "But don't tell any of my friends I forgot, will you? It wouldn't look good, an elephant forgetting."

"You're silly," I said, smiling.

"Yes, you're right, I am sometimes quite silly." Then, looking at the bathtub, his eyes widened. "Could I have a bath? It would be just scrummy." He wiggled his ears. "The very thought is simply delicious."

"Well, I suppose it would be all right, but you must be very quiet."

"Oh this is going to be very exciting, having a bubble bath."

"Well, no blowing bubbles," I said sternly.

"Just a few little ones?" he pleaded.

"No way," I said.

"You're right, not after what happened this afternoon in your gran's kitchen."

I half-filled the bath with warm water and put in some bubble bath. Archie climbed in then stretched out. "Ah, that feels good. Sure beats a water hole in

Kenya, not that I've ever been to one, hee! hee!" he chuckled.

"I'm off to bed," I said. "I'll leave my bedroom light on. Enjoy your bath. There's a towel you can use."

"I hope it's jumbo size," said Archie. "Just kidding! I prefer to drip-dry myself."

I got into bed, picked up a book on elephants and began to read it. I was so happy that my wish had come true, but I was a little anxious at the idea of having Archie around *all* the time, especially when I'd soon have to go back to school after the summer holidays. Still, that was another day's worry. Now, I had my very own elephant in my bathroom having a bath. I couldn't help laughing at the idea.

Suddenly I heard singing from the bathroom.

"Oh, give me a home where the elephants roam, where the gazelles get away from the cheetahs. Where often is heard a discouraging word . . ."

"Oh dear," I said to myself. "He'll waken the whole neighbourhood." Next thing, I heard a loud splash of water like a wave hitting a rock. I hurried out of the room only to bump into Dad, who was standing outside the bathroom door, soaking wet. The elephant stood inside the door with a towel around his waist, looking very guilty.

Dad had a face on him that would turn milk sour. He gritted his teeth and pointed down the stairway. Archie got the message and quickly trampled down the stairs, leaving puddles behind in his wake. The whole house shook as he hurried out the back door to spend the rest of the night sleeping outdoors alongside the dog and cat.

At about eleven-thirty, Mum and Dad went up to their bedroom. Dad first checked my room – just in case the elephant had sneaked back in. All was quiet. I pretended to be sound asleep. Dad checked under the bed to make sure no elephant was hiding there. Then he decided he'd better check Robert's room. He was asleep and there was no sign of Archie.

"It's OK, dear," said Mum, looking out her bedroom window. "It's down there asleep alongside Kitty, Kitty and Ezra."

"Good," Dad said. "Perhaps we can get some sleep. And, hopefully, when I wake in the morning it will be gone and I can put the whole thing down to a bad dream."

"Ted, darling, you're overreacting. It's really very cute, cuddly and highly intelligent," said Mum.

Dad turned in the bed. He punched the pillow several times so he could lay his head on a pile of feathers. "Goodnight!" he growled. Then he switched off the bedside lamp. Just as he began to drift into a pleasant sleep, he became aware of heavy snoring. It seemed to be getting louder and louder.

He switched on the lamp and looked at

his wife, who was wearing earplugs. He shook her shoulder. "I can't sleep with all that snoring. It sounds like a foghorn."

"Now you know what it's like for me," she muttered sleepily, putting back her earplugs.

"Well, it's not me," he grumbled.

He jumped out of bed, pulled up the window and stuck out his head. Now he could see and hear where all the snoring was coming from. That pesky elephant! Even the cat and dog had their paws over their ears.

"Quiet, you . . . you pachyderm!" The elephant suddenly woke up with a start. "That's better," yelled Dad.

There was a loud thud. It was Dad. He

bumped his head on the window frame. He collapsed on to the bed and was out for the count.

"Good night, dear." Mum yawned and went back to sleep.

Outside, the poor elephant couldn't get back to sleep. He tossed and turned. The night was getting brighter, the clouds were gone and a lovely moon shone its silvery light all over the garden. There were lots of stars to be seen.

"Look there," he nudged the dog. "A shooting star!"

"Oh, go to sleep," the dog snapped.

"Here, puss, Kitty, Kitty." He shook the cat with his trunk.

"What is it?" she complained.

"I just can't sleep."

"Try counting mice," hissed the cat.

"I don't like mice," said Archie.

"Try sheep," said the cat.

"That's a very good idea," said the elephant. "I'm glad I thought of it!"

The elephant closed his eyes tightly and began to count sheep. "Oh, there's one, there's another and another. Ah, look at the little black lamb, I hope it's not lost. Hey, stop pushing those lambs, you big bully! Let them get through the gate in their own time. Ah, look, that one's so cute! Hey, look, it's little Bo Peep!"

"Just forget what I said about counting sheep," said the cat, as she tucked her head further under her tail.

*The elephant closed his eyes tightly
and began to count sheep.*

Suddenly Archie heard a footfall on the gravel.

"What was that?" he wondered. There was no answer from cat or dog. He moved his trunk around like a periscope, trying to get a sniff of anything unusual. Then he saw a man dressed in black, climbing out through a window of one of the neighbour's houses, and sneaking across the grass. He then climbed on to the wall and proceeded to get into the Richardson's house through one of the upstairs windows. The intruder was carrying a black sack.

"What's he doing?" wondered the elephant. "He doesn't live here, that's for sure."

With that, a red van slowly pulled up

alongside the house. The window was rolled down and a very sinister man in a peaked cap looked out.

"Listen, dog, Ezra, and Kitty Witty, I mean Kitty, Kitty. There's a man climbing in through one of the upstairs windows."

The dog and cat ignored him.

"Aren't you going to do something?" Archie pleaded.

"Do it yourself," said a very grumpy dog.

Archie began to tremble all over. "Oh dear, I know those men are up to no good. What shall I do?"

He quickly hurried over to my bedroom and tapped on the glass.

I awoke to the sound of the tapping. "I'm sorry, Archie, but you can't come in. Go to sleep."

"Oh, dear," he said. "No, I don't want

to come in, honestly, but I must make a trunk call."

"You're so funny, but it's very late and I'm very sleepy," I said.

"Wakey, wakey, Sophie, there's a burglar in the house. Dear, oh, dear, she's fast asleep again." The front door closed quietly and the man ran towards the van, carrying his black sack that looked even heavier than before.

"I've got the loot, George, let's get out of here."

"Jumping hippos," said Archie. "They're

getting away." Quick as a flash, he was chasing down the street after the van.

Marty, the driver, looked in the rear-view mirror and gasped, then hit the kerb.

"Careful," shouted George. "We don't want to attract any attention."

"But . . . but . . . but . . . "

"What is it?" demanded George.

"We're being chased . . ."

"Oh, no," said George. "Is it the police?"

"No," said Marty. "It's an elephant, and it's pink!"

"Listen, Marty, I told you never to drink before a job is done."

"Look for yourself."

George looked in the side mirror. He couldn't believe his eyes. There

really was an elephant after them, and
it was bright pink. "Step on it!" he
shouted.

"So they think they can get away from
me, do they?" said Archie. "They may
have horsepower, but they didn't reckon
on elephant power."

By now the elephant was gaining on

them. He reached out and grabbed the handle of the back door. The van immediately began to slow down.

"Put the boot down, Marty. Let's burn rubber."

"I'm doing my best," the driver shouted.

The next minute, the two doors of the van were torn off their hinges and crashed into Archie. The van sped off, leaving him sitting on the ground watching stars circling his head.

"That got rid of that pesky elephant," George sniggered.

"Hey, George, what's an elephant doing around here, anyway?" asked Marty.

"How should I know? It probably escaped from the zoo or a circus."

"I think it must have been a circus," said Marty.

"Why do you say that?" George asked.

"Well, because it's pink, and it's flying alongside the van."

Archie smiled as he flapped his ears then flew just in front of the van. The two burglars were so busy looking at the elephant that they didn't notice the police car parked up ahead outside the police station. Crash! Bang! Wallop! George bumped his head on the windscreen and then bounced over the seat, to the back of the police car, landing on the back seat.

When he saw several policemen hurrying out of the police station, the other burglar jumped out of the van and ran down the road as fast as he could. The elephant gave chase, quickly grabbed him by the back of the collar with his trunk, and hauled him to the station. The police could not believe their eyes when they saw the elephant carrying the burglar, kicking and hollering, back to the station.

The police handcuffed the two men and put them in a prison cell.

"At least the sergeant has witnessed this himself," said one policeman to another. "Imagine trying to explain how a pink elephant captured the two most wanted burglars in the city."

They thanked Archie for his great work.

"Ah, it was nothing," he said. Then he lifted up his trunk and moved it about, sniffing the air. "Do I smell doughnuts and coffee?" the elephant beamed. "I simply love doughnuts and coffee." The sergeant told one policeman to order two dozen doughnuts, of every variety they had, for the elephant.

"You're too kind," said Archie, giving

the sergeant a tight squeeze. "I don't suppose I could have a cappuccino as well?" The policemen all laughed loudly.

"Of course you can."

"With plenty of chocolate on top," Archie added.

Later that night I suddenly awoke, and sneaked down the stairs with some supper for Archie, but he was nowhere to be seen. I felt very sad that he would leave without saying goodbye. I assumed that maybe he didn't feel wanted and that was the reason he left. The cat was grateful for the milk, and the dog quickly polished off the slice of bread covered with strawberry jam that I had prepared for Archie.

Next morning, Dad woke to the sound of the doorbell ringing and the doorknocker pounding on the wood. "Who is it at this time of the morning?" he wondered, holding his still-aching head. He looked out the window and could see a police van parked outside.

Mum shrieked, "All my jewellery is gone, and so is the portable TV!"

Then Dad realised that his watch and wallet were gone.

They both hurried down the stairs to open the door. There stood a police sergeant and a detective.

"I believe this pink elephant belongs to you."

Archie waved his trunk and winked. "Hi, everyone!" Robert and I appeared behind Mum and Dad. Dad was ready to throw a wobbly. His wife's precious jewels and the special watch he'd been presented with at the golf tournament were gone, and the police were returning this nuisance of an elephant.

"It's ours all right," I shouted, as I hugged my dear pink elephant.

"Well, we have good news for you," said the sergeant. "This elephant here managed single-trunked . . ." he chuckled, "to capture the two most wanted burglars in the city. So we are able to return your stolen property. And there's a reward of £10,000 put up by the business community, which the elephant wants you to have."

"There goes Dad, fainting again," said Robert as he watched Dad collapse on the carpet.

"Tell me I'm dreaming," said Dad, as he woke up and saw the elephant sitting on the sofa with me, watching an old Tarzan movie.

"Aaahuaaah!" Archie trumpeted, trying to imitate Tarzan's call.

"You're not dreaming, darling," said Mum. "And don't forget that reward we received is thanks to Archie. You'll be able to buy yourself a good set of golf clubs, now. And there are lots of things that need replacing around the house."

"True, true, and it's all thanks to that elephant." Dad smiled broadly and gave me and the elephant a big hug.

"This is so embarrassing," said Archie, "but I love it. In fact, I think there should be a hugging day at least once a week," he added.

All the next week the family, including Gran, went to the circus, the zoo, the cinema, the swimming-pool, and anything Dad thought Archie might like to do. They even played golf together. Dad claimed the elephant helped him improve his golf swing.

Dad brought presents for everyone. It felt like Christmas. Robert got a computer game, Mum got a beautiful necklace, Gran got a new armchair, and I got a big, pink, soft toy elephant. Archie asked if his present could be a donation to the World Wildlife Fund to help his elephant friends in Asia and Africa.

"They probably never, ever get delicious doughnuts or cappuccinos," said Archie.

We all laughed loudly at the idea of all

those elephants sitting about a water hole in Africa eating doughnuts and drinking cappuccinos. Dad agreed to send a generous donation.

A week later, Archie said he had to return to the land of wishes. We were all really sad to see him go but we couldn't be selfish. Someone else might make a wish for a pink elephant and it might come true, as it had for me.

We waited for a warm sunny evening to say our farewell, just after sunset when the clouds were all nice and pinky. We all walked down the pier, Gran included, to say goodbye to dear Archie. After lots of hugs and kisses, he departed. We watched him float away up into the clouds. For a long while, an

After lots of hugs and kisses, he departed.

elephant-shaped cloud floated gently above us. We even felt a few raindrops though it wasn't raining.

So that's the story of how my wish came true.

Sometimes, when the weather is fine, I lie back on the grass and look up at the big fluffy clouds rolling by. Some people see castles in the sky, or dragons, but if I look carefully I can see my very own elephant winking back at me!